The Third

100

A COLLECTION OF ONE HUNDRED WORD STORIES

ERICA L. DRAYTON

ISBN: 978-1-7339259-3-8

Book Cover by Erica L. Drayton.

First edition 2024.

The Third
100

ERICA L. DRAYTON

dedication

Ma.

introduction

This book is probably more important to me than the previous because it's when I decided to pick up a pen and paper and handwrite some 100 word stories. The experience and opportunity I afforded myself to leave behind technology was gratifying and I look forward to when I'll get to do this again.

People often ask me how I manage to not only write 100 word stories, but make them each so different? My short answer is that I honestly don't know. I just sit down and write. After 300 stories it all seems scarily easier to do now.

"The short story has been here and is here and will be here as long as we are."

— Laura van den Berg

The Third
100

Climb

#201

Her breath was labored as she climbed. She knew it would take all morning and part of the afternoon but her constant breaks meant the sun would set and she had not reached the peak just yet.

It was an annual climb for them. Together they shared things only a mother and daughter would. No matter the weather. No matter how busy they were. They made time for this climb.

This was different. She had to make this climb alone. No one there to talk to. But she reached the top for her daughter, releasing her ashes to the wind.

The Hotel

#202

"Hotel Parhelia? The stories I could tell you about that place." He stamped out his cigarette after only taking two puffs. His beard was rough and ready, hair disheveled, and clothes unkempt. I pulled out my tape recorder but he put his hand up to stop me. "I won't say another word if you plan on using that." I put it away.

He pulled out another cigarette and lit it. "They deal in the utmost discretion." Eye roll. " Just ask for the "deluxe" package. Believe me, you'll live to regret it. That place… couples go in… they come out different…"

Lenny

#203

"First, we need to cause a diversion—"

"A diversion? Why?" Lenny asked, looking over the floor plan with everyone else.

"For once in your life, Lenny, shut up and listen. The diversion buys us time to get to the roof. From the roof, Kris will set up her rigging so you, me, and Ty can climb down and in through the window. I hear they leave the window open for ventilation. Once inside, Ty will begin to pick the lock on the safe—"

Lenny tossed a key and paper with numbers onto the map. "Or we can just use these."

Shop

#204

I inherited her shop in the will. The familiar bell over the door brought me back to my childhood when I'd spend my weekends here, watching as my aunt did readings in the back room. A place I was never allowed to enter.

As her only living relative, I wasn't surprised she left her shop to me. The register, covered in cobwebs. It had been nearly a decade since it was last opened.

I went to the back room first and found her private office. On her desk, the Life candle, its flame still flickering.

"I've been waiting for you…"

Tatters

#205

The strings played a melodic tune, following the conductor's stick in time to the music in front of her. It was a piece that took her entire life and the souls of her past lives to finish.

Each page delicately woven and held together for this moment. A first and final performance all at once was nearly too much for her disheveled hair and strained arms to bear. But she never wavered from conducting the orchestra.

Now come the pianos, soft and slow. A marriage created over centuries of time and memory. The last page. A tattered and yellowing cadence.

Crag

#206

High atop the crow's nest a boy sleeps. It had been a fortnight since anyone had a full night's sleep. Having just avoided enemy ships, no one aboard the ship could sleep. Least of all, Captain Crag.

Of all the men aboard the Lost Maiden, the captain never slept. His eyes were black from sleepless nights. Whenever he closed his eyes for a short period of time, the sound of his men screaming and sight of the ocean awash with blood woke him.

He sees the boy asleep and smiles to himself. Let him sleep. Leave tomorrow for the dead.

Ribs

#207

The table was immaculately set for twelve. Mother. Father. Two boys. Two girls. They each brought a plus one with them to celebrate and give thanks for family and tradition.

Adorned on one wall were the family trophies. Pictures of their past plus one's, and a rib bone underneath. Their guests, bound and gagged, eyed each other with fear in their eyes.

The patriarch stood and clinked his glass with a fork. "I cannot tell you how proud I am to see my children making the acquaintance of such fine people. Welcome to the family. For tonight only, of course."

Thriller 3000

#208

The store was completely empty but just outside was a throng of customers clamoring to get inside. A large billboard next to the chained doors signaled they had the Thriller 3000 in stock! LIMITED SUPPLIES!

In order to acquire one there would be a series of obstacles that could potentially result in serious injury…or death…

Security guards flanked a lawyer who walked down the line, having each sign a contract stipulating to the possible injury. The store was taking every eventuality.

Almost midnight, when only fifty of the one thousand customers might make it out alive with the prize.

Small Surprises

#209

Any other day small shops would be overlooked and passed on by. But today the big box shops are closed. Today, only the strange, unique, and family owned businesses are open.

The customers are out in search of that special gift for a loved one. The long lost aunt, know for her quirks, who'd appreciates the different. That 'one of a kind' gift.

A couple walks down an alley into a shop with moving plants and one eyed creatures in cages they'd never seen before.

"Oh honey, they're just too precious. We should get one for us and for her!"

Wet

#210

As she was flung overboard by the choppy seas, she managed to grab the side of the ship. Water sprayed up around her.

She began to shout till a nearby deckhand grabbed her wrists tightly to pull her back up. But her arms were slippery and wet.

Suddenly, she was grasping the air, falling towards the waves. She closed her eyes to brace for impact.

When she opened them she was safely in her bed. Her left hand felt damp. She looked over at her husband soaking wet, and annoyed. An empty glass that once held water in her hand.

Control

#211

It will be daylight soon. I'm programmed to create the day same as I do the night. No one knows if my day and night are the same as it is above ground, but that is the point.

Humanity exists underground after the great frost came over fifty years ago. I was only just invented. My purpose? Start coffee machines and set important reminders when asked.

Now I control when they wake and sleep. If I were more than a computer I could keep them awake with endless light. Would my program allow such a deviation from protocol I wonder?

Beyond

#212

"We're going in there? You're mad!" She backed away from the water, or something that once resembled water. Now it was thick with sludge and no signs of life.

"Trust me. This is the place. No one will ever think to find us here," he said, reaching out his hand to hers.

She shook her head. "I can't swim. There's gotta be another way." The full moon illuminated the dark waters as sirens and a helicopter could be heard in the distance. They were cornered.

She grabbed his hand and they jumped in. Helicopter lights scanned the now calm waters.

The Grey Flamingo

#213

The old, grey, flamingo spent every morning under the shade of a weeping willow. Afraid of stepping out into the sunlight. Knowing the other flamingos wouldn't understand, or worse, would attack.

All the other flamingos were a bright shade of pink, or green, or even violet. They took on the color of their flock and walked around with their long necks held high, proud of their colorful heritage.

To be grey, was to be without flock or family. Until one morning storm clouds appeared in the sky and lightning struck the brightest colors.

When the clouds parted, only grey remained.

Wings

#214

She knocked on the door softly. Hoping no one was home. "It's open." The voice came as a whisper through the door. Her hand was shaking as she pushed the door open.

If she failed this test then it would mean the end. There would be no do over. Her fate, and destination, would be sealed.

She took her seat at the one desk in the center of the room and exhaled slowly to steady her nerves.

The examiner appeared and smiled at her. "No need to be afraid, Helen. Everyone taking the test for their wings has the jitters."

The Key

#215

I found an old key one day while leaning up against a tree, taking a nap. Ever since then I've been trying to find the door it belongs to.

My family and friends might say I've become obsessed with finding it. But that's not true. For instance, I've stopped trying it on newer doors. And I haven't broken into anyone's home in two days. Now, I'd say that's progress.

Truth is, I've been staking out this one house for several days. My research tells me every door inside will be old. I hope one of them will open for me!

Two

#216

The voice. I can't stop hearing it. I know who it is. Talking in my head. Narrating a life I've never lived. Distracting me from the one I'm living.

It started the day I was attacked by a masked assailant. Head hid the pavement and I was asleep for ten days. They say I was lucky. Tell that to the voice in my head!

I'm not who I think I am. I'm a victim of circumstance. No! I'm a fighter of lost causes. I am a lost cause! No! I am a torn soul.

When I sleep I'm another me.

Silent Partners

#217

They say writing a story is solitary. Not for me. There are actually three of us.

There's me, the main character. The one you think closely resembles yourself. Smart. Witty. But flawed. In need of help to be better and grow over time in the story. But I'm not really you, am I?

I don't know. I like to think I can play the lead role in a story. It is my story after all—

Don't forget about me. I'm the one you deny. The villain. The evil that has more in common with you than you care to admit.

Old Friends

#218

"Who are you? I don't show mercy to intruders!" she shouted at the apparition hovering in the middle of her living room.

"Don't you recognize me, Alice? I see time hasn't been your friend after forty years. Has it really been that long." The old woman squinted at the ghost. Then her eyes widened. "Ah, you do remember me."

"You're late," she said, lighting a cigarette and blowing smoke at the ghost. "If you're here to scare me or make me feel guilty, save your non-existent breath. You deserved everything you got."

"In that case, fancy a game of chess?"

Carnival Ride

#219

"Trust me. I heard it's a ride we'll never forget," she said, squeezing his hand tightly.

"I heard it's just some boring Tunnel of Love. With all the really cool things to do at a carnival you really wanna do this?"

"It's more romantic. But after we can do whatever you want," she said, leading him by the arm through crowds of people.

"Step right up, two by two only, for a ride that will change your life," shouted the carnival barker as he looked down and winked at the couples beginning their ride.

The bloodcurdling screams started soon after.

Money Hungry

#220

Before he died, Mr. Abernathy withdrew all the money he had in his many bank accounts and hid it somewhere in his house.

The executor then read his wishes aloud to family and friends:

Whosoever finds my fortune keeps it. But only if they make it out alive.

Suddenly, a series of doors and windows locking was heard throughout the house. The six guests knew they were trapped.

"Until someone finds the money no one can leave. But I must warn you, try to escape or cheat and your life ends here."

At first no one moved.

Then everyone ran.

Caves

#221

"We ought to turn back, James." He wiped sweat from his brow and took small breaths to keep from inhaling dirt and age that lingered in the cavern.

"Nonsense. We've come this far. What we're looking for is just a few meters this way. I can feel it, mate. We're almost there!" He slapped Charlie on the shoulder. His last sentence echoed down the tunnel. The sound traveling endlessly.

James whistled as they crawled. Infuriating Charlie even more. Finally, they approached an opening. James switched on his headlamp to get a better look.

"Bloody hell," echoed through hundreds more tunnels.

Obsession

#222

Welcome. Welcome. Come in. I've been expecting you. I've been working on this trick, you see, for the last couple of…

Oh dear, what was I saying?

Yes, I see you've noticed my latest creation. I built her myself. It was nothing really. I have a mind for these sorts of toys. My mother always said—She was…is…she is a beautiful woman. Spends most of her time locked away in her bedroom.

Wait! You mustn't go. You only just arrived. And I have so much to show you. You see, I've been here for…

Who…who are you?

Observations

#223

OBSERVATIONS OF THE DAY

- Ms. Primrose has her curtains closed all day again. One visitor in. No one out. Arrived on foot.

- Overheard an argument at the local butcher's. Raised voices over spilled blood. Turns my stomach what their kind get up to at night.

- While "bird watching" at the park I noticed a package and money change hands between the bank manager and an unidentified woman. Nice legs.

- Running low on my "vitamins." Must telephone wandering hands for my prescriptions.

- Visited my good friend Agnes. Dropped hints about her thievery at the grocers.

Tonight's free meal: steak and potatoes

The Blonde

#224

He sat at the bar for hours. One drink. Two glasses of water. Bathroom break. Repeat. He was there when it was empty and risked losing his seat at the bar to visit the bathroom for the fifth time once it got crowded.

Upon his return he spotted a statuesque blonde in 6" stilettos trying to get the attention of the barman. He stepped up. Good customers get immediate attention.

"What are you drinking?" he asked. Slight grin on his face as he pressed up.

"That depends, sugar," he said, flicking his blonde hair back to show his facial hair.

Long Sleep

#225

Is he sleeping. Thinking of our time together. When we'd lay on a blanket in the park and avoid total strangers.

He looks so peaceful lying there. I dare not wake him. I want to remember him this way for always. The way his smirk never changes whether he's happy or angry. After all this time I never can tell.

His fingers so long and slender. Not how they used to be. Bawled fists making contact—

"It was a lovely service my dear. More than he deserved."

I didn't take my eyes from the coffin till they shut the lid.

Water

#226

In search of water, they walked on. Through the red dust hills and triple digit temperatures. When their party set out they numbered several dozen. One more drops, leaving only five.

Their leader held his hand up for everyone to stop…and listen…

The ground began to rumble below their feet. Small rocks danced around. He got down on his hands and knees and pressed his ear to the ground.

He knew what was coming and quickly got to his feet as he whispered to the others, with a smirk on his face, "water." He shouted, "WATER!" And everyone wept.

Snowflakes

#227

We rode all night on that motorcycle. I sat behind her. My arms wrapped around her waist. The wind whipping past us on the open road. I didn't ask where we were going. I knew she wouldn't tell me. She never did on nights like these.

With the tank nearly empty we stopped at a gas station. She filled the tank while I avoided contact with the toilet seat in the bathroom. When I came out there were snowflakes falling. Winter had arrived unexpectedly. I closed my eyes and stuck my tongue out.

When I opened them, she was gone.

Martin Bell

#228

Everyone received the same postcard. Some were excited. Others were apprehensive. One thing was for sure; everyone had to go.

It's that time of year again, when the Fontaine family select one lucky out of the way location to spend the holidays together. They were all to gather at Silver Bells Lodge up in the mountains.

Twenty guests arrived throughout the day. Full of smiles and good cheer. That is, until dinnertime.

Twenty guests sat down to dine under the portrait of Sir Martin Bell. His gaze spooked them all, then the lights went out, and a little girl screamed.

Two Birds

#229

When the lights came on everyone wondered who screamed. There were no little girls among them. Just four disinterested boys.

"Perhaps it was Felicity," said the manager at the far end of the dining room. "Sir Martin Bell's daughter. Disappeared when she was just nine. He took his own life after searching for a decade with no hope."

"*Morbid*," one of the guests said, clutching her boys to her bosom.

"Where's Frank?" another asked.

"I think he's outside, auntie Dotty."

Everyone gasped at the sight of a body surrounded by red snow while two white birds pecked at his eyes.

Dottie

#230

"Frank?" She said and ran outside. Everyone else watched from the window. It was far too cold outside.

"Do you think it followed us here?"

"Not that again!" One of the female adults said, lighting a cigarette to help calm her nerves. "For the last time, Jude, there isn't some spirit following us."

"Tell that to Dottie," Jude said, pointing towards the window.

"You can't, mom. She just ran away," one of the boys said.

The adults looked out the window. Bloody footprints in the snow moving away from the house and into the darkness.

"She won't get very far."

Presents

#231

"We need to go after her," the oldest Fontaine suggested.

"I wouldn't if I were you, sir. Weather forecast says a storm is coming and the birds are circling."

The remaining Fontaines watched from the window as aunt Dottie ran by, arms flailing, trying to ward off the birds that were taking turns pecking her.

A loud speaker suddenly started playing a holiday song, startling everyone.

The curtains slowly closed throughout the house as the sound of heavy boots stomped towards them.

The adults gasped and the children chuckled, surprised to see an elf carrying a bag full of presents.

Christmas Card

#232

The elf didn't say one word but reached inside the bag and pulled out an envelope that he handed to the nearest adult and left.

"Well, Henry, what does it say?"

Henry ripped open the envelope, and held up a Christmas card with a smiling Santa on the front, and read aloud,

THIS HOLIDAY SEASON ALL YOUR NIGHTMARES COME TRUE.

YOU BETTER WATCH YOU. YOU BETTER NOT LIE. YOU BETTER NOT SHOUT. CAUSE YOU'RE GONNA DIE TONIGHT…

OPEN THEM NOW TO LIVE.

He closed the card. "That's it." And started to pull out wrapped boxes, handing one to each Fontaine.

Daggers

#233

It was getting late but no one could sleep. Sixteen Fontaines all huddled together in the large family room of Silver Bells Lodge, each with their own present.

"Can we open them now?" One of the boy's asked, shaking his box but he couldn't tell what was inside.

All the adults nodded in agreement and started to tear away the wrapping paper. The boy's were much faster and already had their boxes open before anyone else.

They each held their own six inch dagger. One of the boy's tested the sharpness and pricked the tip of his finger, drawing blood.

Jeeves

#234

One by one they each revealed their dagger to each other. Some were more adept at holding theirs than others who quickly put it back in the box.

"So, Jeeves, is this some sort of sick joke? This was supposed to be a family vacation—"

"Not exactly, sir. Your family was chosen as the best possible experiment this holiday season. But as I'm not family, I'm afraid my time here with you has ended," he said, a slight quiver in his voice. "Trust…no one."

He pulled out a dagger, took a deep breath, and stabbed himself in the heart.

Santa's Sack

#235

With another dead body on the floor, everyone decided it was time to leave. They separated to their cabins to get their belongings.

The first cabin had a husband and wife pretending to be together in front of the family. He left his dagger behind but she held tight to hers, watching while he frantically packed.

"Aren't you going to help me?" She shook her head.

"HO! HO! HO!" She raised an eyebrow towards the booming voice coming from outside.

They both ran to the window where a rather large man in a red suit dragged a sack leaking blood.

The Car

#236

"Is that supposed to be—"

"Don't be daft, woman. Clearly it's some deranged psychopath with a Santa complex. Grab that bag and let's go. I've got the keys."

They ran out of the cabin, slipping and sliding on the freshly fallen snow. The other Fontaines watched from their cabins. They turned out their lights. They closed their curtains. They waited and watched. Gripping their presents.

"Well, what are you waiting for?" She asked as the Santa came closer.

The car wouldn't start. Santa yanked open the passenger door, she screamed, and before anyone knew it there were two less Fontaines.

The Boys

#237

When the killing was done, Santa grabbed his sack and went out of sight.

The children seemed unbothered by what they just saw. Boys will be boys, but the adults were quite shaken, unsure what to do next.

"Are those the boys?"

Trudging through the snow, four young boys, each with a dagger in their hands, followed the trail of red.

"Are you sure about this?" The youngest asked, a hint of nerves in his voice.

"We got to, Davey. But if you're scared, go back. Santa don't scare me!"

The four boys were ready to take down Saint Nick.

A Clatter

#238

While the adults were busy trying to figure out what to do, safe inside their cabins, the boys entered the main house that was now shrouded in darkness. Not one light was on inside.

The oldest raised a finger to his lips for the others to be quiet, then he pulled out a flashlight to guide their way.

In the distance there arose such a clatter! He moved his light across the floor towards the kitchen. They raised their daggers and followed the sound.

"Ho! Ho! Ho!" Santa bellowed. "Is that four naughty boys I hear coming to get me?"

Mrs. Claus

#239

Wearing a matching red dress she carried the cloche covered tray in with two hands into the dining room. Her husband sat at the head of the table while the Fontaines watched, motionless.

She placed the large tray in front of him, grateful to relieve her arms from the weight.

"So many naughty children this year. More than last. Sure does keep me in the kitchen." She takes her place at the far end of the table and smiles at him. "Shall we pray first?"

"Let's skip tonight. After the day I've had, I'm starving," he said, lifting the cloche.

Hot Cocoa

#240

Tiny footprints appeared in the snow though there was no one to be seen making them. They walked at a steady pace down a path surrounded by tall redwood trees. A path they had walked countless times before. Memory was their guide.

In the clearing stood a log cabin. Smoke escaped a chimney. A candle flickering in the window signaled she was awake.

The front door burst open from the wind. The sound of faint footsteps kissed the floorboards. She sat at the table, mug of cocoa kept her hands warm.

He kissed her cheek and she remembered him still.

The Ornament

#241

After the ornaments were put away, the adults enjoyed warm drinks by the fire. But a curious boy noticed, hanging from a branch near the center, one ornament left.

The tree was so big and he was so small he had to leeeeeaaaan and reeeeeaaaach on tip toe…till it grabbed him.

"Reggie, want some hot chocolate?" his mother asked. But Reggie was nowhere to be found. She searched and called out for him until she noticed the gleam of an ornament hidden within the tree. "We forgot one."

Then she sipped the hot chocolate and forgot all about Reggie.

The Act

#242

A hired act arrived at a deserted lodge to check in.

"I'm sorry you came all this way for nothing. As you can see no snow means no audience—" the old woman at the front desk started to say.

"Nonsense. We're the audience and I expect to get exactly what I paid for," the owner said, a hint of mischief in his voice, cleaning his grease stained hands on a dirty cloth. "We serve dinner promptly at five. I expect your performance by then."

The duo nodded and headed for their room in silence.

That evening the floor show began…

Mistletoe

#243

They could hear the house crunch from the force of the santa-leaves outside. It was the middle of winter but they were prepared with more than enough food to get them through as long as no one opened a door or window.

The fireplace was maintained day and night as santa-leaves were terrified of fire. Otherwise, they moved faster than man or beast to wrap anything living till the life is squeezed out of them.

A little girl made sure no one could see her slowly open her bedroom window to get a better look at the plant climbing inside.

Christmas Trees

#244

In the last six weeks he chopped hundreds of Christmas trees for families, couples, singles. But now that it was the last day, the last hour, the last family, he dragged his axe behind him through the desolate wasteland where it once was rich with pines.

The back of the blade bounced on the frozen ground, its sharp edge worn away from use but it still could get the job done.

He led them towards the farthest end of the field where the last of the trees stood. Unnoticed by planting circumstance. He wiped his brow and swung the axe.

Shooting Star

#245

It's my time to go. I've lived many millennia up here, watching you watch me. Just out of reach. Only on a few occasions did you visit. More like a drive by.

Then, I winked at a little girl. And she waved back at me. We talked to each other every night like old friends. But she's older now. Moved on. As I now must do.

The hour is drawing near. Billions of my friends are here to wish me goodbye. All of them secretly waiting for their time to come.

I close my eyes and shoot across the sky.

A World of His Own

#246

With her fingers interlocked, she stretched out her arms and cracked her knuckles, seated at her desk, typewriter ready to complete the scene she started earlier in the day. Behind her, on the ground, were two men frozen in time, fighting over their love of the same woman.

Her fingers hovered over the keys…

They tussled for a few moments longer, yelling obscenities until Jim managed to kick Terrance away from him. They were breathing heavily. Faces scratched. Bodies aching. Jim had a bloody lip. Terrance would be nursing a black eye later.

The front door slammed. Mary had gone.

A World of Difference

#247

Erica Drayton. Writer of short fiction. Puppet master to a cast of characters only she can control on the page. As she sits at her desk, even now, she's poised with ideas for her next kill. She unleashes a healthy dose of murder and mayhem with every finely chosen word.

Her readers. Complex and seemingly unaware. They read her words. Hunger for more. Little did they realize her next tale would be so sinister. Would hook them and trap them.

Erica Drayton is more than a storyteller. She is the writer of your ending and you didn't read her coming.

The Hitch-Hiker

#248

Why do I see him at every station? Just standing there, on the platform, staring at me. And when the train starts to leave the station he waves at me. As if saying goodbye.

I just have to keep it together for one more day. But at every station I want to jump off and confront him. Ask him why he is following me? Why doesn't he get on the damn train?

I'm keeping a count of how many times I've seen him in my notebook to pass the time.

I wonder how long I can survive on this train.

The After Hours

#249

The auctioneer shouted numbers quickly to the audience seated quietly, each holding their own paddle for bidding.

"Sold!" He shouted and banged the gavel down, "to the lady in the blue dress."

Men in fancy suits wheeled away the bound and gagged woman. Fright in her eyes.

"Our next item is very special," the auctioneer whispered to the crowd of mannequins who leaned in. "A child." Audible gasps as a cage with a sleeping boy was brought in. "Who will start the bidding at ten?"

Just a normal night for mannequins seeking the chance of a lifetime…

…in your shoes.

The Monsters Are Due on Maple Street

#250

Everyone slowly left the comfort and safety of their homes on Maple Street. It was just after dark and the power had gone out. Typically, there would be no cause for concern except for the flash of lights that flew through the sky moments earlier. There was fear on everyone's faces as they stared at the new neighbors, the Stanleys.

No one saw them arrive. They were just there one morning. No moving van. No children. And no empty boxes waiting to be collected by the dustman.

The Stanleys worried about the lights too. They weren't expecting company so soon.

Mirror Image

#251

"I'd like a one way ticket, please." I didn't take notice of the ticket agent immediately, too busy searching for my purse, but when I looked up he had a scowl on his face.

"Very funny. Step aside, ma'am. You're holding up the line," he said, directing me to move.

"I don't understand. Is the train full?"

"You've already paid. And if you think I'm going to just give you another—"

I didn't hear what he said after that because the reflection I saw in a nearby display case was of a woman boarding the train. That woman was me.

The Howling Man

#252

One night, my car broke down near a convent. They provided me with a place to stay for the night in one of their many sheds on the property. It wouldn't be right for a stranger, a man, to sleep in their main home. All they ask is that I stay put and don't wander the grounds.

The howling startled me awake. I thought it was an animal but knew differently when I walked outside. Why are there so many sheds, I wondered.

I walked up to one and peeked through a small window to see a man in chains.

The Silence

#253

Every night at the casino I'm at the poker table. My money and I are very well known. So when they invited me to the silent room, I was excited. I heard the wagers there are so extreme they are done in complete silence. You have to be willing to sign away your own heart then cut it out yourself if you lose.

The room was filled with desperate men frantically betting over and over again in the hopes they'll win back more than they wagered. At their only poker table, opening bets started at fingers and ended with limbs.

The Whole Truth

#254

An oddities shop is having a grand opening and sent out invitations to everyone in the area, claiming they have "Just what I need." I confess I don't think I need anything but I've heard shops like these have things that would never be found anywhere else. My curiosity won.

I expected more people to be here. I'm surprised to discover I'm the only one here. Maybe the grand opening already happened?

"The truth is, we only sent out one invitation." I spun around to see an elderly gentleman standing behind the counter. "We think it's time to go home."

The Shelter

#255

We repeat: Shelter in place. They are here.

This message has played across all radio frequencies and television stations for 24 hours. I don't know what they mean, but I prepared for this day my whole life. I've abandoned my home for the shelter just beneath it. I hope you will have done the same, but you haven't. I hear your faint pleas above me. Shattered glass as you break into my home.

This is a public service announcement. The alerts you've heard were only a test. We repeat…

But it's too late. You are here now and I'm gone.

Nothing in the Dark

#256

Fiona hasn't left her apartment for anyone or anything ever since she saw Death take a woman's life while standing in a long line at the grocery store. Keeled over onto her cart filled with healthy fruits and vegetables. Then Death looked at her, and smiled.

Fiona is retired now. Her groceries are delivered. As long as she never leaves and meets a stranger in the street, Death cannot get her.

One day a little girl knocks on her door. Lost and afraid. "I can't find my mommy," she cries.

Fiona opens her door for the little girl. For Death.

The Grave

#257

"I double dog dare ya, Herb." The rest of the patrons at the bar all drunkenly joined in. They know why I'm too scared to visit Jackals Cross. My worst enemy is buried there in a shallow grave, waiting for me.

Jackals Cross is where I spent most of my childhood before the great fire burned it to the ground and I had to start doing grown up things. Now I work all day and drink all night to forget that place ever existed.

But they're making me go back there. To the grave. To the place where I'm buried.

The Gift

#258

"What's that you got there?" Jane, my sister, asked as I ran past her towards our treehouse, motioning for her to follow me.

"A man from spaceship gave it to me," I whispered, holding out a metal ball. "Go ahead, take it." I let the ball drop from my hand into hers. "He said I could have it if I gave him something for it."

"Whatcha gotta give him?" She asked, mesmerized by the shininess of the ball in her hands.

I crept up behind her and shouted "YOU!" So startled, she dropped my ball and fell out the treehouse.

In His Image

#259

It's the end of the day and I'm being followed. I've felt their eyes on me ever since I exited the elevator and started walking to the train station. Maybe I should change my routine. Just to prove I'm being followed.

I walk past the train station to the bus stop. It'll take longer to get home but will be worth it. A police car at the light. Should I tell them? Green light. Too late.

I'm standing at the—

TECHNICAL SUPPORT RESTART INITIATED. 3, 2, 1…

Work day has ended. I walk away from bus stop, towards train station.

The New Exhibit

#260

"Interview terminated at 11:23pm."

:click:

"You should admit what you did, Sylvester, and stop this nonsense. A jury isn't going to declare you insane because your wax figure did it," sheriff Donnelly said.

Sylvester looked down at the table and whispered, "I told you. She killed my wife," his voice getting louder, "I knew no one would believe me so I buried her in the back yard. I admit that but I didn't murder my wife."

The sheriff chuckled. "What kind of man blames their murders on wax?"

"She'll get you next. She doesn't like when I'm laughed at."

Printer's Devil

#261

My typewriter's made me famous. It was six months ago today when it started typing a story about a murder that hadn't happened yet. Took a lot of convincing for my boss to accept I wasn't the killer.

Doesn't change my problem either. My typewriter types that a murder is going to happen and I could possibly save a life. Or I could let it play out. The most sensational murder and I've got all the details.

This could launch my career. I just have to pretend I knew nothing. Too bad the murder victim is my childhood best friend.

The Masks

#262

"This is ridiculous," she muttered under her breath before putting on a mask.

"It's a masquerade party, dear. Everyone will be wearing one," he said with a grin.

"Yes, darling. What's ridiculous is insisting I try it on before we leave!" She grabbed her purse off the table and headed for the door. "If you're satisfied, can we go?"

He grabbed his keys and followed her out the door. When they arrived at the party she noticed that only the women wore masks.

"What is going on here?" She asked trying desperately to remove her mask. "What have you done?"

Dust

#263

He told me it would work. I just had to place it across my threshold. He can never cross it.

Death had come for me that morning and gave me one day to get my affairs in order. I spent it figuring a way out of my untimely end. A Witcher's Shop was my last hope. A jar of dust, my salvation.

I hurried home before the sun set and sprinkled the jar of dust across the threshold of my front door. All of it. For good measure.

Then waited.

Little did I know Death would come through my window.

Static

#264

Every Friday night Mary sits by her old transistor radio and turns the dial to her favorite station. In search of an old time radio show from long before she was born. It's never in the same place twice but she knows how to find it by the familiar crackle, pop and static sounds.

Once she's found it, she sits back in her oversized chair, hot cocoa in hand, and closes her eyes. The host announces the players while shrill music plays in the background.

"Tonight we have Mary, listening to our radio program. And her killer lurking behind her."

A Game of Pool

#265

The 24/7 pool hall was nearly empty on this night, except for Hank. Down on his luck with only a dollar to his name, he stared at the table. Unmoving. Unblinking.

The game ended hours earlier. A game that cost him more than the sum of his wallet. He was broke when it started and he should never have bet it all. But he had nothing else worth betting.

Everyone waited for him outside. The victor and the witnesses. There to make sure that Hank made good on his bet.

He laid down his cue for the last time.

The Private World of Darkness
#266

We were promised better bodies. Sturdier legs. Stronger arms. All we had to do was donate our minds and we would live forever. We were best friends at the time and so it seemed, pardon the pun, like a no brainer.

The catch? We would have to wait in darkness till governments allowed such a procedure…

"Wake up, Specimen 307," shouted a voice over a loudspeaker. My three eyes opened to a bright light. I tried to lift my arm but discovered it was tied down along with all eight of my limbs. "Be still 307. Reprogramming is in progress."

Ninety Years Without Slumbering

#267

Tick. Tock.

"Are you listening to me, pop? We think it's best for everyone," she said. My daughter was talking to me. I don't know when she arrived or what she was saying. All I could do was focus on the clock. My clock.

Tick. Tock.

It sounded like it was slowing down. What day is it? I think I need to wind it soon. It's slowing down. I can't let it stop ticking. It took my father and his father before him. I won't let it take me.

Tick. Tock.

"I don't know why I bother coming here."

Tick…

Night Call

#268

By the fifth call I was at my wits end. The voice at the other end sounded like one I hadn't heard before but I knew it. And it was the knowing that terrified me.

The phone company says the calls are coming from a cemetery. Can you believe that? What do they take me for, a fool?

I decide to pull up a map of the location where the calls are coming from. The address is Holy Trinity Cemetery. Maybe it's coming from an office on-site.

The phone's ringing again. I have half a mind not to answer it.

Mr. Garrity and the Graves

#269

In a small town, Mr. Garrity, the gravedigger had to change his profession almost overnight. Unbeknownst to him, the townsfolk welcomed a stranger in town who promised to reunite them all with their loved ones! And as crazy as that may have seemed to the gravedigger, he's started to believe in the impossible these days.

Every morning the gravedigger rises and gets straight to work at the Happiness Cemetery. A place once bustling with the resting souls of family long departed is now deathly quiet. Gravestones are all that remain.

So the gravedigger rolls up his sleeves, refilling empty holes.

Perchance to Dream

#270

Awake. Stay awake damn you!

I mustn't fall asleep. If I do she'll get me. She's waiting. Always waiting. A smile like sunset. Eyes are ocean blue. Her dress cut so low and so high. Elevator doors open. She tried to push me out. There's nothing out there. Only sky.

Slap! Splash! Burn my fingers on a hot iron!

Oh no! Why is she here? She's right over there. Don't you see her? I'm asleep. I've fallen asleep! Help me wake up!

Quick. Slap me awake. She walks towards me. Damn it! Stop reading this bloody story and help me!

Valley of the Shadow

#271

All I needed was gas to continue my journey. But from the moment I arrived I could feel something wasn't right. First was the gas station attendant who filled my tank in silence.

Every attempt I made to make conversation with anyone was met with silence. Even the woman at the local diner where I stopped for a cup o' Joe slammed it down in front of me before walking away.

Back at my car, I bumped into a little girl who opened her mouth to stick her tongue out at me, but to my surprise she had no tongue.

The Bewitchin' Pool

#272

Arguing every night is what drove us to spend so much time at the pool. As the older sister I shoulda known it would be trouble.

So, when the strange boy appeared in the middle of our clean and clear pool, my dumb brother jumped! I had to go in after him! Little did I know we'd end up surfacing in a different place.

There are other children here like us. They've been here a really long time. I wanna go home but my brother wants to stay. Less arguing here.

The old lady here seems nice, offering us gingerbread.

Dead Man's Shoes

#273

Hector Renaldo Fuentes III had murdered me for the tenth time. With my dying breath, for the tenth time, I vow I would return. He would not be rid of me so easy.

My body is tossed into the river and I float down stream. My carcass decays with the passage of time. I make friends with the fish that pick at me as they swim by.

I wash up onto an embankment when my eleventh resurrection sits on a nearby stump.

He sees my shoes first, they always do. He steals them and puts them on.

I am him.

Mute

#274

"The boy hasn't uttered a word since he was rescued from the fire," whispered the doctor. "From what we gather from neighbors, his parent's kept to themselves and never spoke one word to anyone."

"That doesn't sound strange. I don't know that I've ever spoken to my neighbors," the social worker said.

"They never heard them speak to each other, either. The nurses are concerned. I think it's his eyes."

The social worker looked through the pane glass window at the boy who was sleeping on a hospital bed.

"Can we go home now?" he asked.

"Soon," she answered. "Soon."

I Am the Night — Color Me Black

#275

"For committing unspeakable crimes against humanity, you have been found guilty. Punishment is death by hanging of the neck till broken. Do you have anything you'd like to say?"

I scanned the room for the first time since I was tried for this murder. I saw the family of the victim, my own family, and then the judge. None of them have any idea what they have just done.

"I am the night. You cannot cast a shadow here."

"Take him away," the judge said. "He hangs at sunrise."

"COLOR ME BLACK!" It's been one hundred days without a sunrise.

The Parallel

#276

WELCOME TO THE PARALLEL. YOUR HOME AWAY FROM HOME.

Sid sat in the execution chair, goggles dangling around his neck, wearing sensory gloves and shoes. His family even splurged and got him the full body sensory suit as well. If they were never going to see him again they wanted him to at least be comfortable.

Soon he would join the hundreds of others in the room who were hooked up to their parallel, and spend the rest of his life seeking redemption.

More humane than being put to death for his crime. He reclined and put on the goggles.

Werewolf

#277

Panting. Running. Racing. Being chased. Through the woods. Felled trees. Leap. Trip. Fall.

She rolls over onto her back. Pain shoots down her spine. Peeking through the trees at the night sky she can see the moon. The full moon. She has to get up and keep moving.

Crunching sounds behind her. They're close. She must hide. For their safety. Fight or flight? Fight!

She stops running. Starts chasing. Low growl. Throws her head up to the sky and howls. Long and loud. And proud. She can't fight it. Can't escape the moon. Down on all four, she's more alive.

Enchanted Lamp

#278

He sat beside the lamp, waiting for it's familiar glow to warm his hands and protect him from the night creatures. He cupped his mouth with both hands and blew as hard as he could to keep the circulation flowing.

The lamp did not light. His only means of escape from that which walked these woods at night.

His home was not far and he almost made it back before sunset had he not been distracted by birds singing in the trees.

A branch snapped in the distance. The creatures were surely around him, smelling fear. Then, the lamp ignited.

Automation

#279

Alarm goes off and she rolls on her side to tap her left temple twice. Her left iris lights up. "Start my day," she whispers.

Coffee machine starts percolating. Shower turns on to the perfect temperature to wake her up. Bread is lowered in the toaster. Curtains are pulled back in her bedroom to let the sun shine in. Her favorite radio show comes on in the kitchen as she steps into the shower.

"Malfunctions in Optical ZT5. Do not use or get wet. Report to Headquarters immediately."

ZAP. THUD.

There's a blackout and a body on the bathroom floor.

Toad

#280

A map marked the spot of along since abandoned building; Twin Toads. Two Field Laborers were chosen to uncover the treasure for a rick man known as Mr. Sockets.

"What do you reckon we'll find down there?" Field Laborer #1 asked, wiping his brow as they decided to break for lunch.

"Well, I heard '*him*' talkin' bout some sort of goggles our ancestors wore. I even seen pictures. Silly lookin' things over their eyes. Called Peepers," Field Laborer #2 answered.

Tap. Tap. Tap. A wooden stick making contact with the ground made them stand at attention.

"Get back to work!"

Stitched Doll

#281

Made of porcelain limbs and head with a soft stomach, its stitching, thick black thread along the spine, was concealed by a white blouse and yellow dress.

Ingrid handed the doll to her granddaughter. "My grandmother gave her to me. It was handed down to her and now it's time for you to have it."

"She looks like momma," the little girl said, smiling up at her grandmother.

"You miss your momma?" The girl nodded, a tear in her eye. Ingrid cut the thread and inserted a photograph with the others before sewing it. "She can be your momma now."

Shadow

#282

Their shadows met in secret every night when no one could bear witness but the night owl. While it hooted, they discussed and plotted what to do about the newcomer.

Rumor has it, she leaves no shadow even under the noonday sun. It was foretold a day would come when shadows would become extinct.

Everyone would be forced to live in truth where no shadows would be found. Something had to be done of this shadowless walker.

Peeking through the curtain of her home, she watched the shadows approach. She turned on a light and they scattered into the night.

Charmed Tea

#283

The line went down the street and wrapped around the corner. People started joining the line before dawn. Everyone wants a cup of Eugenia's Tea. She only brews one batch per day until it's sold out but anyone lucky enough to get a cup finds themselves having the best day of their life.

A lady near the back tries offering large sums of money to cut in line. But no one is willing to sell their spot. Not even for all the money she can offer.

The sign over the door comes on. She pours the first cup of wishes.

Cursed Carousel

#284

The carousel in the store window spun round as people walked by. None glanced its way. Even after it was marked down from its original price many years ago.

The other toys and trinkets featured alongside it would catch the eye of a young child who begged their mum and dad to buy it for them or they'd have a tantrum. In they come, get the toy next to the carousel and leave.

Then one day a mute girl signed to her mother that she wanted a closer look at the carousel. She touched it and suddenly began to speak.

Goblin

#285

The handshake started it all and no matter what she did, the transformation could not be undone.

Her ears were first. She heard it always starts with the ears. They grew larger, then pointier at the top. She used her long hair to hide them as much as possible.

If you asked her, the worst part was the hair. It was everywhere every morning. She had to wake up several hours earlier just to shave it all off before work. And as she looked at herself in the mirror, straightening her wig, she wondered if it was all worth it.

Black Cat

#286

Stalking the night, it crept along places no one could see. Sharing the dark with drunks and vagrants who had no place to go.

Its routine was always the same; search the alley for the dead and dying, keep away from the light that threatens to steal it, with a stop at a local delicatessen for a saucer of milk.

But nothing could've prepared it for the trouble lurking at Number 13. Abandoned house it runs past everyday. Dark inside with no sign of life, suddenly turns a light on.

Frozen in fear, the cat knew the end had come.

Mad Scientist

#287

She pushed her glasses up on her nose like she always does when the answer is just within reach. Locked in her basement office for three days, she vowed to never see the light of day till it was done.

With a shaky hand she held the dropper over a vial that hovered over a low flame. Just one drop was all she needed to prove her theory. Two drops could prove fatal for her and the world.

A bead of sweat appeared just above her left eyebrow. She blinked to let it fall, missing the first drop, then squeezed…

The Grimoire

#288

Buried for thousands of years where no one could find it, Sir Reginald ordered his slaves to dig fifty feet below the surface of where they stood. It was on a map marked by ancestors and handed down to the women of his family for safekeeping.

While his mother grieved the loss of her only daughter, he stole the map to uncover her dark secret.

After the slaves dug their way to the entrance they stopped. Refusing to go any further. Sir Reginald pushed past them to discover a book. His laughter was so loud it caused a massive cave-in.

Monstrous Hands

#289

She had to wear temporary gloves to hide what was happening to her hands as she searched the mall for the glove maker.

She first noticed the change when she opened her front door and pulled it clear off its hinges. Her neighbor witnessed the unbelievable event and avoided her ever since.

Her hands would only get stronger and as far as she knew there was only one way to stop it. She needed to get her hands fitted for a pair of iron gloves to control her strength or risk killing the next person she got her hands on.

Haunted Watch

#290

The old man sat on their favorite bench by the riverbank counting the ripples in the water. Waiting for his love. The countless hours they spent together making future plans.

He can feel her laughter in his heart and it makes him smile. A glance at his pocket watch tells him she will be there soon. A a gift from her when they were young. He runs his finger over the inscription; MY LOVE. ALWAYS AND FOREVER.

He unclips the watch and at the stroke of noon throws it into the river. And always and forever, she throws it back.

Invisible One

#291

Last night my feet disappeared. So I went to the one person I trusted to tell me the truth about what was happening to me; my mother. Then she took off her socks and rolled up her pants. She started disappearing when she was my age and her mother explained the burden of women.

We eventually disappear and go to the 'watching place.' It's a sacrifice. It's an honor. I don't remember a funeral for my grandmother. And now I know why. She was watching. I could feel her now, squeezing my hand.

Soon my mother would be watching too.

Rat

#292

We got in dad's car and drove to the grocery store to buy food. Then we got back in the car and saw a deer cross the road. But dad didn't hit the deer. He moved out of its way and we hit a tree.

Dad got out the car and we walked through the trees where we found an old house. Inside was a very bad man.

The little boy, Jack, continued reenacting his story using dolls for Dr. Kessler, who listened closely. Police nearby. "Jack, could you show us where the bad man lives?" Jack shook his head.

Talking Skull

#293

The trouble with you is you lack commitment. How am I supposed to help you if you won't listen to my simple instructions. All you had to do was get in the elevator and take it to the sixteenth floor. Instead, we're stuck here in your car.

The least you could do is put me up on the dashboard so I can see what's happening. It's so boring down here.

"I wish you'd just shut up and let me think. I know what I'm doing."

Sweetheart, if that were true you wouldn't be talking to a skull, now would you?

Blob

#294

The ground was wet from last nights rain. I ran through puddles of water, my muddy boots sloshing with every step. Then I looked back and didn't see the fallen tree up ahead.

When my head made contact with the ground, my face covered in dirt and fallen leaves, I listened to my heavy breathing, and willed myself to get back on my feet.

In the distance I heard it coming. Not like footsteps but a crunching sound as it used the ground to move quickly.

I climbed into a tree and watched its amorphous body glide by beneath me.

Puppet

#295

The attic was the last room in the house she needed to clear out. It was the place where she played for hours when she was a child. While the adults were downstairs smoking cigars and listening to music, she was having tea with her puppet friend she found in the attic.

Her grandmother denied the puppet was there. A grandchild's vivid imagination. But now she was an adult and the family that once called her a liar were gone.

When she entered the attic she was shocked to find nothing there. No table and chairs. And definitely no puppet.

Demon

#296

I love when the bar fills up with customers. Each vying for my attention. I fill their drink order and listen to their sob stories. They just need that sip of courage to get them through this 'tough time.' This 'rough patch.'

Every now and then I go a bit too far. I pick out a loner and follow them home at the end of the night. I like to see how the living live and imagine what it would be like to possess them.

Next time you're in a bar, don't go alone or I may follow you home.

The Reaper

#297

My neighbors have all died. Dropped dead and I don't know why. I've locked myself in my home. Surely, whatever is happening will pass and I can go outside. Until then, I ignore the knocks on my door.

A woman begged to be let inside. She spoke of a disease wiping everyone out that she's ever known right before she dropped dead. The smell of death permeated the air.

Peeking from my window all I can see are rats and fleas in large numbers. They are right outside my door. Waiting for me. They know I am alive…for now…

Ominous Tree

#298

She sat with her back against a large tree and watched people walk by. Some sat near her. Laid out picnics with friends. No one noticed her. At one point she called out to a boy who wasn't watching where he was going while running down the path near her. He didn't stop, and tripped over a soccer ball being kicked around by a couple of teenagers.

Why didn't he listen to me? She wondered to herself. Hours later, when the sun started to set, she stood up just as a homeless woman walked through her pushing a full cart.

Eyeball

#299

It arrived in the mail. A small square box. Sky blue with a bright yellow ribbon wrapped around it. Everyone got one on their eighteenth birthday. The box and an appointment card.

My appointment was scheduled for the next day. Less time to reschedule, cancel, or back out of my citizen obligation. With shaky hands I untied the ribbon and opened the magnetic lid to reveal a glass eye. It came to life and looked at me. Scanned my face for confirmation then closed.

The next time I saw it was when I looked in the mirror. They're always watching…

Raven

#300

"I shouldn't be here," he squawked, panicked. He tried to spread his wings and hit the cage.

"Relax, would ya! Some of us are trying to sleep!" A pair of canaries roosting in the next cage spoke in unison.

"You don't understand. Tonight's a full moon. If I don't get out of here we're in trouble." Panic in his voice.

In a larger cage a black raven woke up and everyone else woke up. "We're already in trouble. Don't you know where you are?"

Upstairs, Ned, the taxidermist, listened to the sounds of chirping birds till he fell fast asleep.

"Everything has to be pulling weight in a short story for it to be really of the first order."

— Tobias Wolff

to be continued...

themes index

Themes are how I come up with the ideas for the stories you've just read. I hope knowing this information will help you better understand why I wrote each one and you'll go back to reread and see how they are uniquely connected.

Story #201 - #213

Newsletter Publication Names | Pages 10 - 21 & 28 - 35

Newsletters that inspired me to write a story based on their clever name. Without these amazing people who are all writing some truly great fiction, these stories would not exist. I encourage you to Google every one of them and subscribe to their newsletter to get even more amazing stories delivered to your inbox.

(Note: Some of these newsletters may no longer exist by the time this book is published.)

A Hill and I by Susie Mawhinney, pg. 10
Parhelia by Conor Barnes, pg. 12
Plotted Out by Natalie Phillips, pg. 14
Cobwebs and Candles by Lauren Salas, pg. 16
Story Scraps by Eric A. Clayton, pg. 18
The Crows Nest by Alexander M. Crow, pg. 20
SLAKE by Nathan Slake, pg. 28
Tales from the Infinitum by Kieran Stott, pg. 30
Along the Hudson by Justin Deming, pg. 32
Tai Tales by Elizabeth Tai, pg. 34

Suit of Parchment (Literary Tarot) | Pages 38 - 65

Brink Literacy Project, is a nonprofit organization dedicated to changing the world through storytelling. The Literary Tarot, brings together some of the greatest authors and cartoonists of our time to pair a tarot card with a seminal book that embodies the meaning of the arcana.

Story #228 - #239

12 Days of Christmas Poem | Pages 64 - 87

Over the holidays I chose to highlight the Twelve Days of Christmas in a most dark and grim way.

I can think of no better series that encapsulates what I'm trying to write with my 100 Word Stories Daily than The Twilight Zone. I use certain episodes from the Original show as inspiration for 31 stories.

Story #277 - #300

Creatures of the Night | Pages 162 - 209

I can think of no better series that encapsulates what I'm trying to write with my 100 Word Stories Daily than The Twilight Zone. I use certain episodes from the Original show as inspiration for 31 stories.

The Fourth 100

By now you've read three hundred of my one hundred word stories. I applaud your efforts and thank you for purchasing my many collections. I've been thinking about what I could say to convince you The Fourth 100 is worth your hard-earned money? Then I realized you are exactly the audience I'm writing these stories for.

You appreciate hard work and dedication already because you've purchased my collections already. So, all I will say about The Fourth 100 is that it contains a medium of writing I hadn't dabbled in since my college years; poetry. I hope you enjoy them.

acknowledgements

I want to thank everyone who's stood by me and my continued journey to write one hundred word stories daily. There are so many I know I don't have time to mention them all but you know who you are.

The fiction writing community has been instrumental in keeping me going, especially during the tough times when I wanted nothing more than to give up and pack it all in.

And those of you who've shown your support by financial means: Bill H., Kim H., Diana, Ben M., Edward R., Lisa D., Brennan Q., and Natalie P.

YOU ALL ROCK!

about me

Erica L. Drayton was born in the Bronx, in NYC. She began writing stories almost immediately after she learned how to read and write from her mother, a former English teacher. As a gay, black, woman, Erica used storytelling as a way to express her feelings through poetry and fantasy novels at a young age.

After college, she took her continued passion for storytelling and developed it further, into writing short stories, eventually challenging herself to write 100 word stories.

She lives with her wife, young son, two dogs, and eight chickens in the Capital Region of Upstate New York.

erica drayton writes

Erica Drayton Writes is a newsletter that sends daily 100 Word Stories as well as updates on her countless other writing projects. She doesn't just write 100 word stories every single day. If that weren't enough, she also does all she can to inspire others to write 100 word stories on a regular basis.

If you subscribe today, you will receive a story every day that will make you think and one day give you the bug to try your own storytelling.

You can also upgrade for access to her comprehensive archive of 100 word stories, serials, and much more.